Family

FAMILY MOVIE NIGHT SOIREE To-Do LIST

☐ 1. Design an *Elegant Coiffure*

(that means create a SPARKLY movie-star hairdo)

☐ 2. Transform backyard into breathtaking outdoor amphitheater

(that means put up decorations)

☐ 3. Make a STUNNING debut

(that means LIGHTS, CAMERA, ACTION)

KEYANA LOVES HER FAMILY

Written by
Natasha Anastasia Tarpley

Illustrated by
Charnelle Pinkney Barlow

LB

LITTLE, BROWN AND COMPANY

New York   Boston

Some people say it's better to start small. . . .
But I'm Keyana McGee, and I love **BIG** ideas!

Sometimes big ideas
need a lot of work....

But the best ones are always worth it!

Tonight is family movie night, and I have a *new* **BIG** idea: a backyard movie soiree!

I've already invited my family members to this fantastical affair. Now it's time to do my hair!

**I brush
  and twist
    and poof my curls.**

I save the best part for last: my jewel-encrusted princess tiara, elegant and tall.

"Ta-da!" I rush to show Mama my creation. "Isn't this the most spectacular movie-star hairstyle you've ever seen? Perfect for a soiree!"

"It absolutely is!" Mama smiles. "You know, Keyana, a soiree is a pretty big job for one glamorous superstar alone. Perhaps I could lend a hand?"

"Don't worry, *dahling*," I say. "I've got everything under control."

First, I set up *all* the snacks in the backyard by myself:
lemonade in fancy movie-themed paper cups, buttery popcorn,
and sweet chocolate candies of all kinds.

Next, I hang colorful streamers and shimmery
balloons while Mama and Daddy set up the chairs,
the movie projector, and the screen.
Suddenly, I hear footsteps behind me. . . .

It's my little brother, Miles—with *my* balloons!
"I. Am. A. Green-horned. Snorkelbot," he says.
(That just means he's wearing a dinosaur hat, a snorkel mask,
and his robot costume from two Halloweens ago.)
"Balloons. Help. Me. Fly. To. Planet. Snorkelbot!"

"Those are for my soiree!" I say.
But just as I reach for them, a gust of wind blows them
up,
   up,
      up into a tree, too high for me to reach.

Daddy rushes over with his ladder and rescues *some* of them.

"Next time, ask your sister before you take something, okay?" Daddy says.

Miles nods. "Sorry, Keyana."

"Thanks, Miles—I mean, Green-Horned Snorkelbot. I know you didn't mean it."

"*BRAIN FLASH!*" Miles yells so loudly it makes me jump. "You can use my spaceship kite instead of the balloons!"

That *would* look pretty cool.

"Bravo!" Daddy cheers. "I know you always do big things, Keyana, but sometimes Mama and I, and even green-horned snorkelbots, can lend a hand."

"I'll keep that in mind, but right now I have to finish getting ready!"

Before I know it, my stupendous work is done and my guests are here.

There's my great-aunt Ruby,
the fashionista, and her glamorous
Great Dane, Daschall . . .

my uncle Charles,
the brilliant baker . . .

my uncle Dave,
the jazz musician . . .

. . . and my five favorite cousins.

Last to arrive are Grandpa Jack, Grandma Anna, and their scaredy-cat, Jasper.

Finally, it's time to start the show!
"Lights,
   camera,
      action!"
The crowd cheers, I bow, and the movie begins.

Everything is going great—until halfway in.
And the trouble starts with two of my five
cousins, the twins.

"You took the cookie with the most chocolate chips," one twin yells at the other.
The noise startles Jasper the cat, who leaps onto the fence and pops a balloon.
Daschall barks and runs right into the snack table,
    which knocks down the screen,
        which hits the movie projector with a loud *crash!*

Everything goes dark.
"My backyard movie soiree is ruined!" I wail.

I run inside and cry on my bed.

Soon, Mama comes in and squeezes me tight.

"I know this was not the soiree that you planned,
but you did something better."

"I did?" I wipe my face and sit up.

"Absolutely! You brought us all together."

Suddenly, another **BIG** idea pops into my head!

I race to the backyard.

"What if we make our own movie instead?"

Grandpa Jack is the first to speak. "That's a brilliant idea, Keyana!"

Great-Aunt Ruby says, "Daschall and I will create the costumes from whatever you have around."

"And I'll provide the sounds," Uncle Dave says, holding up his trumpet.

"We want parts, too!" my five cousins clamor.

"But the green-horned snorkelbot gets to be the villain," Miles growls, "though green-horned snorkelbots are actually very nice."

"I'll whip up some homemade ice cream for dessert," Uncle Charles offers. "Now, where do you keep the ice?"

Mama sets up the props, and Daddy films everything on his phone.
Everyone is having so much fun. No one wants to go.
But one by one, they all head home.

"That was the best movie night ever!" I say as Mama combs my hair before bed.

"See what can happen when family members stick together?" Mama smiles.

"You're right," I say. "I don't have to do *everything* by myself, especially when my family is here to help."

That night, before I close my eyes, Miles
sneaks into my room.

"These are for your next soiree," he says,
"in case your other balloons fly away."

I love my family, I think as I drift off to sleep.

And I don't even mind my green-horned
snorkelbot brother's cold, smelly feet.

To my niece and nephew, Kimora and Naveen. May you always follow your hearts, and may your BIG ideas change the world. —NAT

To my amazing family. Thank you for your continuous support. —CPB

About This Book

The illustrations for this book were created digitally and finished with a handmade watercolor texture overlay. This book was edited by Alexandra Hightower and designed by Véronique Lefèvre Sweet. The production was supervised by Patricia Alvarado, and the production editor was Jake Regier. The text was set in Charcuterie Serif Regular, and the display type is Daft Brush Text.